A Note from Mi...
PIGS, PIES, AND PLENTY OF PROBLEMS

Hi! I'm Michelle Tanner. I'm nine years old. My dad and I baked a yummy apple pie for the father-daughter bake-off. But here's the problem. I wanted our pie to look extra special. Dad said it was perfect and told me not to mess with it. But I tried to decorate it anyway, and knocked it to the floor. *Splat!* Now I have to make a new pie all by myself, *and* keep it a secret. That's going to be really tough, because my house is full of people.

There's my dad and my two older sisters, D.J. and Stephanie. But that's not all.

My mom died when I was little. So my uncle Jesse moved in to help Dad take care of us. So did Joey Gladstone. He's my dad's friend from college. It's almost like having three dads. But that's still not all!

First Uncle Jesse got married to Becky Donaldson. Then they had twin boys, Nicky and Alex. The twins are four years old now. And they're so cute.

That's nine people. And our dog, Comet, makes ten. Sure, it gets kind of crazy sometimes. But I wouldn't change it for anything. It's so much fun living in a full house!

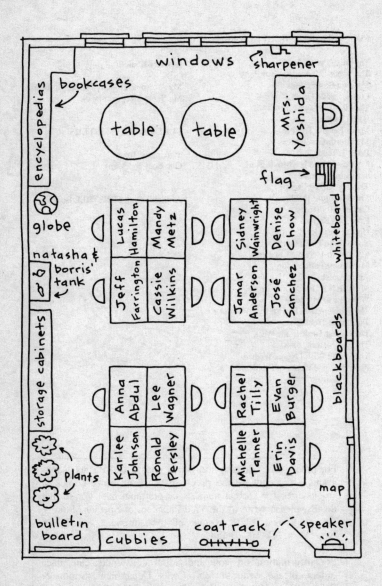

FULL HOUSE™ MICHELLE novels

The Great Pet Project
The Super-Duper Sleepover Party
My Two Best Friends
Lucky, Lucky Day
The Ghost in My Closet
Ballet Surprise
Major League Trouble
My Fourth-Grade Mess
Bunk 3, Teddy and Me
My Best Friend Is a Movie Star!
    (Super Special)
The Big Turkey Escape
The Substitute Teacher
Calling All Planets
I've Got a Secret
How to Be Cool
The Not-So-Great Outdoors
My Ho-Ho-Horrible Christmas
My Almost Perfect Plan
April Fools!
My Life Is a Three-Ring Circus
Welcome to My Zoo
The Problem with Pen Pals
Tap Dance Trouble
The Fastest Turtle in the West
The Baby-sitting Boss
The Wish I Wish I Never Wished
Pigs, Pies, and Plenty of Problems

Activity Books

My Awesome Holiday Friendship Book
My Super Sleepover Book

FULL HOUSE™ SISTERS

Two on the Town
One Boss Too Many

Available from MINSTREL Books

For orders other than by individual consumers, Pocket Books grants a discount on the purchase of **10 or more** copies of single titles for special markets or premium use. For further details, please write to the Vice President of Special Markets, Pocket Books, 1230 Avenue of the Americas, 9th Floor, New York, NY 10020-1586.

For information on how individual consumers can place orders, please write to Mail Order Department, Simon & Schuster Inc., 100 Front Street, Riverside, NJ 08075.

FULL HOUSE™

Michelle
and Friends

PIGS, PIES, AND PLENTY OF PROBLEMS

Cathy East Dubowski

A Parachute Book

A MINSTREL® BOOK

Published by POCKET BOOKS
New York   London   Toronto   Sydney   Tokyo   Singapore

A MINSTREL PAPERBACK *Original*

A Minstrel Book published by
POCKET BOOKS, a division of Simon & Schuster Inc.
1230 Avenue of the Americas, New York, NY 10020

A PARACHUTE BOOK

Copyright © and ™ 1999 by Warner Bros.

ISBN: 0–671–02152–4

First Minstrel Books printing September 1999

10 9 8 7 6 5 4 3 2 1

Printed in the U.S.A.

Chapter 1

♥ "Thanks for the ride, Dad!" Michelle Tanner told her father, Danny. She gave him a quick hug and hopped out of the minivan. It was Wednesday. Michelle had missed the bus by a second. So, Danny had to drive her to school.

"Don't forget this." Danny handed her a shiny red apple. Last week the whole family went apple-picking. Michelle wanted to bring the best one to her fourth-grade teacher, Mrs. Yoshida.

"Good luck, pumpkin!" Danny closed the door and pulled away.

Michelle heard the school bell ring. She saw Jamar Anderson and Jeff Farrington race toward the building.

Oh, no, she thought. I can't be late. Not today!

Today was the day Michelle's class got to pick new seats. Sometimes Mrs. Yoshida liked to change everyone's seats. She said it made things more interesting.

Michelle brushed her strawberry-blond bangs out of her eyes. She hung on to her pink and blue backpack and ran to Room 402. When she stepped inside, she couldn't believe her eyes. Her class looked like a farm!

A scarecrow stood next to the globe in the back of the room. Pumpkins and baskets filled with vegetables were placed on the shelves— right next to an aquarium and a hamster cage. Photos of different animals covered the bulletin boards. Small stacks of hay lay beneath the blackboard.

A stuffed pig with a name tag that said BUDDY sat at the corner of Mrs. Yoshida's desk. Buddy looked as if he was reading a copy of *Charlotte's Web*.

Michelle laughed. She knew one of the main characters in the story was a pig named Wilbur.

The students' desks were set up in groups of four. Almost all the seats were already taken.

Michelle crossed the front of the room to Mrs. Yoshida's desk. She pulled a shiny apple out of her pocket and placed it on the corner. "Good morning," she told the teacher.

Mrs. Yoshida wore blue denim overalls and a red checked shirt. She had short black hair, shining dark brown eyes. "Why, thank you," she said. "I love apples."

Cassie waved to her from the back of the

class. "Michelle! Over here! We saved you a seat!"

Cassie and Mandy sat side by side, with Lucas Hamilton in the third desk.

Michelle hurried toward the empty seat. Just before she reached it, Jeff Farrington slid into the chair.

"Hey, that's my seat!" Michelle exclaimed.

"Really?" Jeff looked all around it. "I thought it belonged to the school."

Lucas laughed. "Good one, Jeff!"

"Come on, Jeff," Mandy pleaded. "We were saving that seat for Michelle."

"Tough luck," Jeff said. "I can't leave poor Lucas alone at a table full of *girls.*"

Lucas gave him a high-five.

"Please, Jeff?" Michelle begged.

"Here's an empty seat." Mrs. Yoshida pointed toward a desk closer to the front. "Okay, everyone," the teacher called out. "Let's get settled."

Michelle sighed and took the empty chair across from Erin Davis. She had a friendly face with lots of freckles.

Evan Burger sat next to Erin. Evan was pretty messy. His new desk already needed to be cleaned out!

The girl sitting next to Michelle was new to the class. She had shiny brown hair that hung past her waist. She had big blue eyes. Her cool clothes looked expensive.

"Hi, my name is Michelle Tanner. You're new, right?"

The girl glanced at Michelle. "I just changed schools, if that's what you mean. My name is Rachel Tilly."

Rachel was tall, slim, and athletic-looking. Michelle wondered if she was any good at sports.

"I used to go to a private school," Rachel went on. "It was much nicer than this one. I was captain of the basketball and soccer teams. I had lots of friends, and I made straight A's."

"So what happened?" Evan asked. "Did they kick you out?"

Erin clapped her hand over her mouth and giggled.

Rachel gave Evan a mean look. "My teacher told my dad that I was the best student she'd ever had—that I was *perfect*. But my father thought I should know what it's like to go to public school. With ordinary people . . . like *you*."

Evan scowled at her, then doodled something on his desk.

"Evan was only kidding," Michelle told Rachel. "What you said was kind of mean."

Rachel shrugged. "So what?" She pulled a notebook from her backpack.

Rachel seems perfect at everything, Michelle thought. Everything *except* being nice. She glanced over at Mandy and Cassie.

She wished she was sitting with her best friends.

Mrs. Yoshida called out the roll.

Then José Sanchez raised his hand. "Mrs. Yoshida, how come there's farm stuff all over the room?"

"I'm glad you asked, José." Mrs. Yoshida grabbed a straw hat from her desk and plopped it on her head. "We're going to be talking about farms this week. As you all know, this weekend is the big harvest celebration. Raise your hand if you'll be going to the fair with your parents."

The whole class raised their hands and cheered.

Every year Fraser Street Elementary School hosted a big harvest festival. It was held in a town just outside San Francisco. People came from all over to see the animals, enter in contests, and eat great food.

"Okay," Mrs. Yoshida went on. "Raise

your hand if you're entered in a festival contest.

Michelle stared at the apple on her teacher's desk and smiled. She was in the father-daughter apple-pie-baking contest. And Michelle knew she couldn't lose.

Mandy's hand shot up. "I'm going to be in the pig-calling contest," she announced proudly.

"You know how to call a pig?" a girl in the back asked.

Mandy shook her head. "Not really. I saw someone do it on TV once. It looks like fun!"

"Hey, Mandy," Jeff said. "Maybe you can practice on Mrs. Yoshida's pig, Buddy!"

"Would you like to try?" Mrs. Yoshida asked Mandy.

"Sure." Mandy walked to the front of the class. She took a deep breath. Then she leaned back and hollered, "Heeeeere, piggy, piggy, piggy. Soooo-weeeee!"

The kids in the class laughed and clapped.

"All right, Mandy!" Michelle cheered.

Next Mrs. Yoshida called on Cassie.

"I'm going to be in the bubble-gum-blowing contest," Cassie told the class.

"What's that got to do with a harvest festival?" Ronald Persley wanted to know.

Cassie shrugged. "Beats me. They have a watermelon-eating contest, too. But I didn't think I could eat much watermelon. Blowing bubbles is something I *know* I can do."

Mrs. Yoshida called on a girl near the back of the room. Her name was Karlee Johnson. "I'm not in a contest, but my uncle owns a farm a few hours away," Karlee told the class. He's going to show some of his animals at the fair, and I get to help."

"What kind of animals does your uncle raise?" Mrs. Yoshida asked.

"Cows mostly," Karlee replied. "But he also has goats, some chickens, a few horses, and some pigs. My favorite is a pig called Curly Sue. I named her myself."

Michelle raised her hand. "I'm entered in the father-daughter apple-pie-baking contest with my dad. It's a family tradition," she explained. "Both my sisters, D.J. and Stephanie, won a blue ribbon when they were my age. And I'm going to win one, too. My dad is an awesome cook!"

"How exciting," Mrs. Yoshida said. "Do you have a secret family recipe you're going to use?"

Michelle knew that they would be using Grandma Tanner's secret recipe. She smiled mysteriously and said, "My lips are sealed. But I picked the apples myself."

"Now, that's *really* baking from scratch," Mrs. Yoshida replied. "Well, Michelle. Good luck!"

"Thanks!" Michelle said. But she didn't really need luck. Nobody ever came close to beating the Tanners in a baking contest. Winning was going to be as easy as pie.

"What are you doing at the harvest festival, Rachel?" Mrs. Yoshida asked.

Whatever Rachel's doing, I bet she'll be *perfect* at it, Michelle thought. She'll probably win a blue ribbon, too.

Rachel stood up and grinned at the teacher. "I'm in the father-daughter apple-pie-baking contest. Just like Michelle." She looked down at Michelle and added, "Won't that be fun, Michelle? We'll be in the same event."

Michelle looked into Rachel's big blue eyes. Rachel was smiling. But it wasn't a friendly smile. It was a *fake* smile.

Michelle gulped. "That will be . . . just *perfect*," she forced herself to say. Maybe she can't cook, though. She can't be great at *everything*.

"Do you have a secret family recipe, too?" Mrs. Yoshida asked Rachel.

"No," Rachel replied. "My dad makes up his own recipes."

Yes! Michelle thought. Sounds like a dad who doesn't know his way around this kitchen!

"You see, my dad is a chef," Rachel explained. "He just opened his own bakery." She smiled at Mrs. Yoshida.

Michelle gulped. "You're dad owns a real *bakery?*" she asked Rachel.

Rachel nodded. "And he makes the coolest, fanciest apple pie in the whole world. He learned at a famous cooking school in *Paris.*" She leaned close to Michelle. "Do you still think you're going to win that blue ribbon, Mi-*chelle?*"

Michelle sank down in her seat. She wasn't so sure anymore.

Chapter
2

♥ "Dad, we have to bake our pie tonight," Michelle said at the dinner table that night. "Right after we're done eating."

"I'm not sure we want to do that," Danny replied. "Don't you want the pie to be as fresh as possible? We already have to bake it a night early because I'll be out of town on Friday."

"When I was nine, we didn't bake our pie until the very last minute." D.J. buttered an apple-fritter biscuit. She was eighteen years old and in college. "And look what hap-pened . . . we won!"

"But you guys don't understand," Michelle said. "There's this new girl at school. She's in the contest. And her father's a real baker."

Thirteen-year-old Stephanie was sitting next to Michelle. "But you have all those fresh apples we picked." She rubbed her shoulder and groaned. *"Nine whole bags* of them."

"That's what happens when the Tanners go apple-picking," Uncle Jesse said. "We mean business!"

Michelle grinned. Uncle Jesse was right. It was her idea to pick fresh apples for the contest. The whole family had helped. And that's a lot of people!

There was Michelle, her father, and her two sisters. Then there was Joey Gladstone, her dad's friend from college. Joey moved into the Tanner home a long time ago. He came to help out after Michelle's mom died. He lived in an apartment in the basement.

Uncle Jesse moved in back then, too. Now he lived on the third floor with Aunt Becky and their four-year-old twins, Nicky and Alex.

The only ones in the family who didn't go apple-picking were Comet, the family's golden retriever, and Michelle's guinea pig.

"Apple-picking was a wonderful idea," Aunt Becky told Michelle. "We really should make this a regular family outing. Even the twins had a great time."

"Yeah," Uncle Jesse said as he wiped Nicky's hands with a wet washcloth. "But they're going to smell like apple juice until they're six."

Michelle laughed.

"Maybe I'll use the extra apples in my act." Uncle Joey was a stand-up comedian. He got up and started juggling three apples. "If I get hungry for a snack . . ." He grabbed one apple out of the air and took a bite. Then kept on juggling. "I won't have to stop the show!"

Michelle laughed. "But what about Rachel? She's—"

"Don't worry about a thing, Michelle," Danny said. "The Tanners always do their best. That's why we always win." He left the table and went into the living room. Seconds later, he returned with a big photo album. He sat down at the table next to Michelle and opened the book. Together they turned the pages.

Michelle watched as photos of holidays, birthdays, and vacations flipped past. In some pictures her father had long hair and wore funny clothes. Her big sisters looked like skinny little kids. At first there were no photos of Michelle. But then she did show up—as a baby in diapers!

Her father stopped at a page with a photo of

Danny and a young girl with long blond hair. The girl smiled proudly. A blue ribbon dangled from the apple pie she held.

"That's me!" D.J. giggled as she looked at the picture.

"D.J. was nine—almost ten—when we won our first blue ribbon," Danny said.

Michelle didn't remember that day. She counted on her fingers. "I was just one year old then."

Danny nodded and turned to the next page.

Michelle's dad was in this photo, too. The girl in the picture wore her hair in two neat braids tied with red bows.

"That's when Dad and *I* won the blue ribbon," Stephanie said. "I was nine, too."

Michelle sort of remembered that one. She was four back then.

The next page in the album was empty. "Look, Dad," Michelle said. "There's a photo missing."

Danny smiled and shook his head. "No, pumpkin. Nothing's missing. I've been saving that page in the album for a very *special* picture. Our picture. When *we* win the blue ribbon! Now that you're nine, it's your turn to continue the tradition."

Michelle touched the blank page. She imagined her picture there. She would be smiling proudly beside her dad. Can I do it? she wondered. She wanted it more than anything. She wanted to follow in her sisters' footsteps and bring home the blue ribbon.

But when D.J. and Stephanie won, they didn't have Rachel Tilly and her dad in their contests. They weren't up against a baker who learned how to cook in Paris.

Michelle would have to do something extra special for this apple pie-baking contest—or else her goose was cooked!

Chapter 3

♥ Michelle stared at the recipe her father had propped up on the counter. The card was yellowed with age. At the top of the card were the words: GRANDMA TANNER'S APPLE PIE.

We're doomed, Michelle thought glumly.

It was Thursday evening. Danny would be out of town on business on Friday. So, Michelle and her dad were baking their apple pie a day early. The pie they were entering in the harvest festival on Saturday.

Michelle thought about perfect Rachel and

her perfect dad. Mr. Tilly probably wears a perfect white chef's hat when he's cooking, she said to herself.

She frowned at Grandma's recipe. A couple of old spills dotted the worn card. Someone had used a small strip of yellowed tape to repair a tear.

How can we win with this old thing? Michelle worried.

It was an old-fashioned recipe from an old-fashioned lady who never even went to cooking school.

But how could she tell her dad that without hurting his feelings? "Um, Dad?" Michelle began.

Danny tied a white apron around her. "Yes, pumpkin?"

"Maybe we should try a new recipe," she suggested.

Danny opened a cabinet and took down a large white mixing bowl. "But why? Grandma Tanner's pie worked for me and D.J.— and then again with me and Steph."

"That's just it," Michelle replied. "You already won with it twice. It's yesterday's news."

Danny laughed. "Why mess with success?"

"Because it's old success, Dad," Michelle argued. "We need something . . . something *new and improved*."

"Sweetheart, things don't always have to be new and improved to be good," he said.

"But, Dad, you don't understand what we're up against." She explained again about perfect Rachel and her perfect chef dad.

"Michelle, you've eaten Grandma Tanner's apple pie a hundred times," Danny said. "Isn't it the best?"

Michelle thought about it. The apple pies her dad made were delicious. But delicious enough to win a blue ribbon?

"Please, Dad, can't we try something new?"

Danny pointed to Grandma's recipe card. "Read."

Michelle sighed and read the list of ingredients: flour, salt, vegetable shortening, and ice-cold water.

Borrr-ring, Michelle thought.

"How about adding chocolate chips?" she suggested.

"To apple pie?" her dad exclaimed. "We're not going for the humor award. Let's stick to Grandma's recipe."

"I know!" she said. "Let's change the ice water."

"What can you use instead of ice water?" Danny asked.

"Apple juice," Michelle replied.

"But, Michelle, that's—" Her dad stopped talking. Then he smiled. "That's . . . interesting."

Her father opened the refrigerator and pulled out an unopened bottle of apple juice. He held the measuring cup while Michelle poured the flour. Danny dumped the flour into a bowl while Michelle mixed in chilled vegetable shortening.

"Now add the apple juice, a tablespoon at a time, so the dough won't be too wet," Danny told her.

Michelle mixed the apple juice into the flour mixture.

"Don't mix it too much," her dad warned. "That will make the crust tough. We want ours to be light and flaky."

It was hard work, but fun, too. At last her dad began to roll out the dough. He patted it into a big lump, then split it in two. He set one lump aside.

"What's that for, Dad?" Michelle asked.

"Grandma Tanner's recipe—like lots of recipes—makes enough crust for two pies," Danny explained. "In the old days especially, when they had larger families, good cooks rarely made just one pie at a time."

"What do you mean, the *old* days?" Michelle joked. "We've got a pretty big family now."

Danny laughed as he showed Michelle how to roll out the dough. Then he put a small amount to the side.

"What's that for?" Michelle wanted to know.

"So we can taste our apple-juice experiment—without cutting the pie," Danny explained.

Danny showed Michelle how to line a pie pan with a circle of dough. Next they made the filling. Danny peeled and sliced the apples. Michelle stirred them in a bowl with sugar, cinnamon, nutmeg, and butter. She dumped the filling into the pie pan.

Michelle laid some dough for the crust on top. Then Danny poked a circle of small holes in it with a knife.

Michelle's mouth watered. She couldn't wait to taste it!

Danny made a little pie with the small ball of dough and a few tablespoons of filling. "We can taste this at the end to make sure everything turned out okay," he told her.

Then they popped the pies into the oven to bake.

Michelle gave her dad a floury high-five.

"Good job, Michelle," her father said.

The tiny pie was ready sooner than the big one. Danny pulled it out of the oven. When it was cool, they each took a bite.

"Mmmmm!" Michelle moaned.

Danny tasted a bite. Then he smiled. "Michelle, I'm impressed. The hint of apple in the crust really adds flavor to the pie. In fact . . ." He took another bite. "It's the best pie I've ever tasted. Thanks to you, Michelle." He gave her a hug. "Grandma Tanner would be proud."

Michelle beamed. "We make a great team."

"You bet!" her father said. "And with this pie—we're definitely going to carry on the

family tradition and win another blue ribbon!"
He put the extra dough and filling in the refrigerator. Then he and Michelle cleaned up.

Michelle couldn't wait until Saturday.

But then something popped into her mind.

Rachel Tilly's face. Smiling a fake smile at
Michelle—as if Rachel had just won a blue
ribbon.

Michelle stared at their pie, cooling on a
rack on the counter. Sure it tasted good. But
was it special enough?

"Wait a minute, Dad!" Michelle called as
her father started to leave the room. "We're
not finished."

Danny laughed. "What do you mean? The
pie is done."

"But we've got to add something to it. Like
. . . like chocolate chip cookie dough. Or
M&M's." Michelle began to pace the room.
"Maybe we could decorate the crust with little
cutouts of apple trees and sprinkles and—"

"Michelle," her father said, "our pie is fine."

"But, Dad—"

"Now, Michelle, it's natural to get cold feet right before a contest," he told her. "But a good cook has to have confidence in his cooking. And I do. Our pie is perfect."

As perfect as Rachel Tilly's? Michelle wondered.

"But maybe I could just—"

"Don't touch it," Danny said firmly. He placed it on top of the refrigerator. Then he covered it with a white cloth napkin. "Now I'm going to go upstairs and pack my overnight bag." He gave Michelle a kiss and left the kitchen.

Michelle sank down at the table and sighed.

Then she heard a knock at the side door. Michelle answered it. Cassie and Mandy stood outside.

"Are you ready to work on our great grains report?" Cassie asked Michelle.

"Oh, yeah." Michelle let her friends inside. "Dad and I just finished baking our pie. I almost forgot about our homework."

"So, how did the pie come out?" Mandy asked.

"Do you need us to taste test it for you?" Cassie said with a grin.

"No, it tastes okay," Michelle replied, closing the door. "But it will never beat Rachel Tilly's pie."

"What about adding chocolate chips," Cassie suggested.

Michelle shook her head. "My dad already said no to that."

"Well, let's see the pie. Maybe we can come up with another idea to make it special."

"I can't," Michelle replied. "Dad told me not to touch it."

"We'll just look at it," Mandy said. "We won't touch it."

Michelle thought about it for a second. She really wanted the pie to be special. Besides, what could happen if she just showed it to her friends?

"Okay." Michelle pulled a chair over to the refrigerator. She climbed onto the chair. Then she stood on her toes and grabbed the pie.

But then Michelle lost her balance. Before she could do anything, the pie slipped right out of her hands and—

Splat!

It smashed to the kitchen floor!

Chapter 4

♥ "Oh, no!" Michelle covered her face with her hands. Maybe it wasn't as bad as it sounded.

She peeked at the floor. It was.

The beautiful pie that she and her father had made together lay splattered across the kitchen floor. "All our hard work—ruined because of me!"

Michelle jumped down from the chair and dropped to her knees. "What should I do?" she asked her friends.

"Maybe we can piece it back together," Mandy suggested. "You know, like a jigsaw puzzle."

"Maybe." Michelle scooped up some pie in her hands. Some of the filling oozed out through her fingers. She and her friends tried to smoosh the pieces of pie back into the pie plate. Then Michelle tried to pat it into shape.

"No way." Cassie groaned. "This pie is history!"

"And Dad and I can't bake another one. It's too late tonight, and he won't be home tomorrow. I knew I shouldn't have touched the pie. I knew it!"

Mandy ran to the swinging door that led into the living room. "Michelle! Quick!" she whispered. "I think somebody's coming!"

Michelle grabbed the pie. She climbed on the chair and placed the pie back on top of the fridge. She covered it with the cloth napkin. From the outside it looked the same as before.

Michelle hopped down and grabbed some paper towels. "Help me clean this up, you guys!" she whispered to her friends.

"Michelle," her father said as he came into the kitchen. "What are you doing?"

Michelle glanced up at Danny and smiled as brightly as she could. "Uh, just cleaning up a little spill, Dad!"

Danny nodded his approval as he poured himself a glass of water. "That's my girl! The best cooks run a clean kitchen."

He smiled at Michelle's friends. "So, did you tell Cassie and Mandy about the pie we baked?"

"Oh, yeah," Michelle said nervously. "They know all about it."

Danny shook his head. "I'm so excited. It's going to be such a thrill to win the father-daughter apple-pie-baking contest for the third time—with my third daughter. How lucky can a father get?" Then he left the room.

Michelle felt terrible. What in the world was she going to do now?

Chapter
5

♥ "Michelle? Are you with us this afternoon?" Mrs. Yoshida asked the next day at school.

"Huh?" Michelle looked up from her *Charlotte's Web* book.

"I just asked you to read the next page," the teacher told her.

Michelle couldn't believe it. She was so worried about the apple pie contest that she hadn't even heard Mrs. Yoshida.

Rachel raised her hand. "I'll read next, Mrs.

Yoshida." She smirked at Michelle. "We're on page thirty-seven."

"Go ahead, Rachel," Mrs. Yoshida said.

Michelle glanced at her watch. Ten minutes to three. She couldn't wait until school was over.

Michelle didn't have the heart to tell her dad that she'd ruined their apple pie. There was only one thing she could do. Bake another pie. Fast. In secret.

Cassie offered her kitchen to do the baking. Her mom said it was okay.

The bell rang. Cassie and Mandy rushed to Michelle's side. "Meet us in a half hour," Cassie whispered. "For *you know what.*"

Michelle nodded. Then Cassie and Mandy left the classroom.

"See you at the contest, Michelle," Rachel said. She gathered her things and walked over to Mrs. Yoshida.

"Good luck." Evan pushed in his seat. "I hope you win."

"She will," Erin said. "Remember those cupcakes she and her dad made for the bake fair last year? They were awesome."

"Thanks." Michelle slipped her books into her backpack and took a deep breath. "Okay, Michelle," she said to herself. "It's time to bake a blue-ribbon pie."

"You are the best friend ever," Michelle said to Cassie. "And so are you," she added to Mandy.

Michelle unloaded the apple pie ingredients onto Cassie's kitchen counter. "I tried to find the leftover dough and filling," Michelle told her friends. "There should have been enough to make another pie." She shrugged. "I guess my dad threw it out."

"That's okay," Mandy said. "Maybe it will be better anyway if we make everything fresh."

Cassie's mom came in and sliced the apples for them in her food processor.

"Whoa, that was quick, Mrs. Wilkins," Michelle said.

Cassie's mother smiled. "I'll leave you girls to make the dough and filling. But be sure to call me when you're ready to bake. I don't want you using the oven without me."

The girls promised, then went to work. Michelle opened a big bag of flour.

"Here, piggy-piggy-piggy!" Mandy started doing her pig call. She grinned. "I hope you guys don't mind. I've got to keep practicing for the harvest festival."

Crack! Cassie popped a great big bubble of gum. "Me, too."

"That's okay with me," Michelle said. "Besides, I don't think you guys should actually *help* me make the pie anyway. It might not be fair."

Michelle dug around in the bottom of her paper bag. "Uh-oh."

"What's wrong?" Mandy asked.

Michelle groaned. "I forgot to bring Grandma Tanner's recipe." She looked in the bag again. "I thought I put it in here."

"Can't you just remember what you did when you made it with your dad?" Cassie asked.

Michelle leaned on the counter. "Maybe. I remember all the ingredients: apples, sugar, flour, some spices." She pushed up her sleeves and started to work.

But how many apples was it? Michelle couldn't remember. And was it one half cup sugar? Or one and a half cups of sugar?

Michelle shrugged. The more sugar the better!

The crust was the hardest part. With her dad to help her, it had seemed easy. Now she couldn't seem to roll it out right. First she rolled it out too thick. It didn't cover the pan. Then she rolled it out too thin. When she tried to put it in the pan, it tore. So she had to ball it up and roll it out all over again.

"Maybe you need more flour," Cassie said. She opened a flour tin and scooped out some in a measuring cup. Then she sneezed. Poof! A white cloud flew up and dusted her face.

Michelle laughed. "You look like a clown!"

"Oh, yeah?" Cassie said. Then she scooped up some flour in the palm of her hand and blew it at Michelle.

"Hey!" Flour flew into Mandy's hair, too. Laughing, she grabbed a handful of flour. "How would *you* like white hair?"

"Flour fight!" Michelle laughed and tossed a fistful of flour at Cassie.

The girls giggled and screamed as they threw flour at one another. It was so much fun. It really cheered Michelle up.

"Girls? What's going on?" Mrs. Wilkins stood in the doorway.

The three girls froze.

"Uh, sorry, Mom," Cassie said. "It was my fault."

Mrs. Wilkins brushed some flour out of her daughter's hair and tried hard not to smile. "Good cooks always clean up as they go," she said.

"That's what my dad says," Michelle mumbled.

"We'll clean up, Mrs. Wilkins," Mandy promised.

The girls swept and wiped up the flour. Then went back to the pie.

"Are you sure you don't want us to help?" Cassie asked her.

Michelle nodded. "It wouldn't be fair. I've got to do this all by myself."

At last she got the crust rolled out and into the pan. She poured the filling inside. It didn't look exactly like the filling she and her dad had made. But Michelle figured that didn't matter.

Just like before, Michelle had enough dough and filling for two pies. So she decided to bake them both. That way she could give one to Cassie as a thank you for using her kitchen.

At last the pies were ready for the oven. Mrs. Wilkins came in to help.

"Don't forget to set the timer," Cassie's mom reminded Michelle. "You don't want your pies to burn."

Michelle picked up the timer. But how long should it bake? Without the recipe, she couldn't be sure. Michelle just guessed.

"Come on," Cassie told her friends. "Let's go watch TV while we wait."

When the timer rang, Michelle, Cassie, and Mandy ran into the kitchen.

With Mrs. Wilkins's help, Michelle used oven mitts to remove the pies from the oven. Then she set them on the table to cool.

The girls stared at the pies. Steam rose from the crust.

Michelle was so excited. The crust looked golden brown and delicious!

"Mmm, it smells wonderful," Mandy said.

"Congratulations," Cassie said. "You did a great job."

When the pies were cool, the girls sat down at the table to taste the extra one.

Cassie leaned forward and sniffed. "I can't wait to taste it!" she said excitedly.

Michelle cut three slices and placed them on plates.

"You try it first," Mandy insisted. "Since it's your pie."

"Okay," Michelle said. She stuffed a big forkful of apple pie into her mouth and chewed. Then she frowned.

"What's the matter?" Mandy asked. "Isn't it just like your dad's pie?"

"No!" Michelle cried. She spit the pie onto her plate. "This pie is totally gross!"

Chapter 6

♥ Michelle burst into tears. "I must have messed up the recipe," she told her friends. "This is awful. My pie will never win a blue ribbon!"

"Maybe it's not so bad," Mandy said gently.

"Here, let's taste it," Cassie said.

Both girls took a bite of apple pie. Michelle watched hopefully. Maybe I'm just being too tough on myself, she thought.

But her friends' faces told her all she needed to know.

The pie was awful!

Mandy politely spit her bite into a napkin. "Well, it's not that bad. . . ."

"Forget it, Mandy," Cassie said. "We're her friends. We should tell her the truth." She turned to Michelle. "You were right, Michelle. It's gross."

Mandy began to clear a space on the table. "We'll just have to start over again. And this time, we'll help you. Maybe we can—"

"Forget it," Michelle said glumly. "Thanks for trying, guys. But let's face it. I can't bake a blue-ribbon pie by myself—even if there was time. And there isn't. I have to be home soon."

"But, Michelle, what will you do?" Mandy asked.

Michelle shrugged. "There's only one thing I can do. I'll have to tell my dad when he gets home tonight."

Michelle helped her friends clean up the

kitchen. She thanked Mrs. Wilkins. Then she left to go home.

With each step, Michelle walked slower and slower. She lowered her head and sighed. How was she ever going to tell Dad about this? she wondered.

"Hey, watch where you're going, Mi-*chelle*," a voice said.

"Huh?" Michelle glanced up. Rachel Tilly was standing there with her hands on her hips.

"You almost bumped into me," Rachel said. Then she flipped her silky brown hair behind her shoulder. "Have you made your pie for the harvest festival yet?"

Michelle wasn't quite sure how to answer that. She'd baked a pie twice. But she still didn't have a pie for the festival. "Well, not exactly . . ." she began.

"Don't bother," Rachel said. She unchained her bike from the bike rack in front of a store. "You'll never win. Not against me and my dad." She hopped on her bike. "See you later."

Michelle thought she heard Rachel whisper "loser" before she pedaled away.

I am *not* a loser, Michelle said to herself. She turned and continued on her way home. And I'm not going to let my dad down, either, she thought. I have to figure out a way to win that blue ribbon.

Sniff, sniff. Suddenly the air seemed filled with the sweet smell of fresh-baked apple pie. Was it Michelle's imagination?

Michelle followed the scent to a small bakery. A little neon sign in the window said HOME-BAKED PIES.

Don't even think about it! Michelle warned herself.

But she was desperate. Without another thought, Michelle ducked into the shop. Hmmm, the pies looked pretty much like the one she and her father baked. And she had just enough money saved from her allowance . . .

The next thing Michelle knew, she was walking out the door with a plain white shopping bag—a freshly baked apple pie inside.

Once home, Michelle slipped inside the front door. She needed to put the pie in the kitchen. But she could hear Joey and Uncle Jesse in there, talking and laughing.

Instead, Michelle sneaked the pie upstairs. Luckily, D.J. and Stephanie weren't around.

She dashed into her room and closed the door.

Safe! Michelle thought.

She sat on her bed and stared into the shopping bag.

And started to feel guilty.

Can I really do this? she wondered. Can I really cheat to win a contest?

Chapter
7

♡ Michelle shook her head. I can't pretend that this is my pie, she told herself. It's just not right. She placed the white bag on the floor.

Then she heard her father come upstairs and go into his room. Dad's back from his trip, Michelle thought. Tell him, she said to herself. Tell Dad everything.

Michelle went to find her father.

At the door to his room she stopped. He was talking on the phone. Who was he talking to?

"I'm so proud of Michelle," she heard him say. "She's a natural in the kitchen. Like father, like daughter, I guess. The pie she and I made turned out perfect. And she really had a great idea for changing the recipe." He listened for a moment. "Oh, no. I can't tell you that. That's our secret!" He chuckled. "I can't wait till Saturday. It's going to be a special day when we win that blue ribbon."

Michelle's heart sank. How in the world could she tell him she ruined their pie? How could she tell him to forget their blue-ribbon dreams?

Michelle could see no way out.

Later that night, when everything was quiet, she sneaked down to the kitchen with her store-bought pie.

I feel like a thief in my own house, she thought. Except she wasn't sneaking something out. She was sneaking something in!

She climbed onto a chair and looked under

the linen napkin on top of the refrigerator. The ruined pie was still there.

Quickly, she switched the store-bought pie for the other one. Then she put the ruined pie in the white shopping bag.

Michelle couldn't resist. She stuck her finger into the smashed pie and tasted it. Yum! It was so delicious! But that only made her feel terrible.

Sadly, she picked up the white shopping bag and slipped out the side door. She buried it way down in the garbage can, where no one would ever see.

When she came back inside, Stephanie was making some hot chocolate in the microwave. "Michelle," she said. "Want to watch that new comedy show on TV with me? Dad said we could see it if we finished our homework."

Michelle didn't feel like watching a funny TV show. "I don't think so."

The microwave pinged and Stephanie carefully took out her mug. "Come on. I'll make you some hot chocolate."

"Thanks," Michelle said. "But I—I've got something I need to do." Then she ran upstairs to her room.

She tried to read. But she couldn't keep her mind on the story. She took out her markers and paper and tried to draw. But the only picture that came to her mind was Rachel Tilly holding a blue ribbon. And her dad's disappointed face.

At last she gave up. She took a quick bath, brushed her teeth, and went to bed early. She was glad Stephanie wasn't there yet to ask her what was wrong. Soon her father came in to tell her good night.

"In bed already, pumpkin?" he asked with a soft laugh. "You must be nervous—like me. I always get nervous before a cooking competition. Don't worry, it's perfectly normal."

Danny neatly tucked in her covers. Then he

leaned over and gave her a kiss. "I'm really proud of you, sweetheart. See you in the morning."

Michelle gulped as her father left the room. She felt horrible—as if a big rock were sitting on her chest.

She hugged her favorite stuffed animal, Mr. Teddy. "Do you think my fake pie will fool the judges?" she asked him. But Mr. Teddy kept his thoughts to himself.

I hope it works—for Dad, she thought. I don't want to let him down.

Chapter
8

♡ Michelle woke up—and groaned. It was Saturday—the day of the harvest festival.

A pillow landed with a soft plop on her head.

"Wake up, sleepyhead," her sister Stephanie called out. "You can't win a blue ribbon in your jammies!"

I can't win a blue ribbon no matter what I wear! Michelle thought. She dressed quickly and hurried downstairs.

Everyone in the house was gathered in the

kitchen. Danny was serving a quick breakfast of muffins and juice. Aunt Becky and D.J. were double-checking their cameras.

"Okay, kiddo," D.J. told Michelle. "We've got a lot of family pride riding on this."

"Yeah," Stephanie teased. "You'd better win—or forever live in shame!"

"Hey, lay off, guys," Joey broke in. "You'll make her nervous. Besides, Michelle already knows that if she doesn't win, she might as well not come home!"

Everyone laughed. They were only teasing.

But Michelle couldn't even smile. She was the only one who knew the truth. The only one who knew about the phony pie.

"Nervous?" Aunt Becky asked her.

"Sort of," Michelle replied. Terrified was more like it!

Danny handed her a small red cooler. "Hold on to this," he told her. "Our pie is in there."

Everyone piled into the family van and drove to the harvest festival. Aunt Becky and Uncle Jesse took the twins to some rides set up for little kids. Stephanie and D.J. decided to visit the crafts exhibits. Joey went to get something to eat.

Michelle followed her father into a tent. He took the cooler from her and pulled out the pie. Then they headed toward the judges' stand.

Michelle looked around for her friends. Cassie and Mandy were supposed to meet her there. But Michelle didn't see them.

The judges' table was covered with pies— lots of pies. More pies than Michelle had ever seen at one time. Enough pies to feed her whole school!

"Hi, Mi-*chelle!*" someone said.

"Oh, no," Michelle muttered. She knew that voice.

Rachel Tilly waved to her from the other

end of the table. Her father was carefully setting out their pie.

"Good luck, Michelle," Rachel said sweetly as she and her father passed by. Then she whispered so the dads couldn't hear, "You'll need it!"

Michelle walked to the other side of the table. She took a closer look at Rachel's pie. Oh, no, she thought. Her pie is beautiful. The crust was golden brown. It was covered with fancy cutouts and decorations. Not only that, but it was in a beautiful antique pie plate.

It looks like a picture from a magazine, Michelle thought with a sigh. No—it looks like a picture on the *cover* of a magazine.

Michelle felt worse than ever.

Her father's arm slipped around her shoulders. "Don't worry, pumpkin," Danny whispered in her ear. "Pies are just like people. It's what's inside that counts."

"Michelle!" Cassie and Mandy called at the same time. They walked up to the judges' stand.

"How did you get a pie in the contest?" Cassie whispered.

Michelle sighed. Then she quietly told her friends about the fake pie.

Cassie put her hand on Michelle's shoulder. "Don't worry. It will work."

"My mom went to the quilt exhibit," Mandy told Michelle. "Let's walk around the fair."

"Can I, Dad?" Michelle asked her father.

"Sure," Danny said. "The judging doesn't start for a while."

"Let's go look at the animals," Mandy suggested as they headed out of the tent. "Maybe I can practice my pig calling."

"Okay," Cassie said around a mouthful of gum.

"Careful, Cassie," Mandy teased. "You don't want to wear out your mouth before your bubble-blowing contest."

Soon they found the big barn where the animals were kept.

Inside, there were several pens of animals. Kids and their parents were having fun petting and feeding them.

Michelle waved to her classmate, Erin Davis. Erin was feeding a carrot to a beautiful brown and white pony.

"Look!" Cassie said. "There's Karlee from our class."

The three girls hurried over to see her uncle's animals.

Michelle had trouble with the fence latch at first. But at last she got it open, and they went inside.

"Whoa!" Michelle exclaimed. There were pigs, horses, chickens, cows—not the kind of animals a city girl like Michelle usually got to see!

"My uncle lets me name them," Karlee said. "This is Chocolate Chip the horse. That rooster is called Cluck Kent. And these cows are Milky Way and Moooonbeam."

"Wow, those are great names," Michelle said.

"Thanks," Karlee said. "Do you like animals?"

Michelle nodded. "I have a dog named Comet and a guinea pig, too. But he doesn't have a name."

Mandy laughed. "She's had that guinea pig for months, and she still hasn't named him."

"I haven't been able to think of a good one. Maybe you can help me," Michelle said.

Karlee thought a minute. "How about Sunny?"

"That's cute!" Cassie cried.

"I love it!" Michelle told her friend. "That's what I'm going to call him. Thanks, Karlee."

"You're welcome. Now come meet Curly Sue," Karlee said. "You can practice your pig calling on her, Mandy."

Cassie and Mandy followed Karlee, but

Michelle stayed behind. She couldn't keep her mind off the apple pie contest.

She patted Chocolate Chip's nose. "I shouldn't have been horsing around with the pie my father and I baked," she told him.

"Am I a pig for wanting to win the blue ribbon no matter what?" she asked a few piglets.

Cluck Kent the rooster clucked at her.

"I know, I know," Michelle muttered. "I shouldn't have been such a chicken about telling my dad."

The animals seemed to stare at her as they mooed, oinked, neighed, and squawked.

And Michelle knew at once what she had to do.

I can't go through with the contest, she decided. What if we win with a pie we didn't bake? D.J. and Aunt Becky will take pictures. Dad will put one in the album. Right next to the photos of D.J. and Stephanie winning their blue ribbons. I'll have to look at it for the rest of my life. And every time I see it, I'll remember how I won my blue ribbon by cheating.

She had to tell her dad. No matter how much it hurt him to hear the truth, she knew it was worse to enter a lie.

She ran over to Cassie and Mandy.

"I can't go through with it," she told them. "I'm going to take the fake pie out of the contest. I'm going to tell my dad the whole truth."

"Oh, Michelle," Mandy whispered. "Are you sure?"

Michelle nodded. "It's the right thing to do."

"Well, you'd better hurry," Cassie said, looking at her watch. "It's almost time for the judging to begin."

Michelle and her friends hurried out of the animal pen. Michelle was the last one out. She fumbled with the latch on the fence. Then she dashed off with her friends.

"Come on, Michelle," Mandy said. "Cheer up." She hollered out one of her pig calls to try to make her laugh. "Sooooo-weeeeee! Here, piggy-piggy-piggy!"

"I think you'll win with that call," Cassie said.

"Really?" Mandy said. "Do you think it will work on a real pig?"

Cassie started to answer. But a shout interrupted her.

"Nooooo! Wait! Stop!"

"That's Karlee," Cassie said.

Michelle and her friends whirled around.

The gate to the animal pen swung open.

"I think your pig call works great," Michelle told Mandy. She pointed. "Look!"

"Oh, no!" Michelle gasped.

Curly Sue was running straight for them!

Chapter 9

♥   "Help!" Karlee yelled. "Runaway pig!"

"Oink-oink-oink!"

Michelle's hands flew to her face. "I must not have closed the gate right."

"Let's get out of here!" Cassie cried.

"Catch her!" Karlee shouted.

Cassie squealed as Curly Sue raced past them.

Michelle felt torn. It was her fault Curly Sue was on the loose. But she needed to find her dad before the pie contest started. Should she help catch the pig instead?

"Don't worry, Michelle," Mandy told her. "You find your dad. We'll take care of Curly Sue."

"Speak for yourself," Cassie said. "Curly Sue looks a lot bigger now that she's out of the pen."

"Give me a break." Mandy pulled Cassie out of the barn. She let out another "Soooo-weeeee! Here, piggy-piggy-piggy!" Then she and Cassie raced after the pig.

Michelle ran for the tent where the pie contest was about to take place. Where was her dad?

Michelle looked around. Oh, no! He was talking to Mr. Tilly!

Michelle ran over and grabbed her father's arm. "Uh, hi, Dad. Can I talk to you?"

"Sure, honey," Danny said with a smile. "In just a minute. Mr. Tilly was just explaining to me his method of making low-fat bran muffins."

Michelle stood on tiptoe. "It's really important," she whispered into her father's ear.

Danny looked puzzled, then worried. "Excuse me, Jim," he told Mr. Tilly.

Michelle noticed Rachel staring at them. Michelle walked a few steps away. Her father followed.

"What is it, Michelle? Are you all right?"

"I'm fine," she gasped. "But . . . well, maybe we should quit the contest."

"What?" her father cried loudly. "Quit the contest? But—but why?"

Michelle glanced around and blushed. People were staring at her and her father.

Rachel leaned forward, trying to hear.

Michelle gulped. She wanted to tell dad everything. But not with everyone watching. But she couldn't let her father go through with the contest. Michelle had no choice.

"I—I—" she began.

"May I have your attention, please!" the head judge called out.

Everyone in the tent hushed instantly.

Wait! Michelle wanted to scream. But she knew it was too late.

"We have decided on the five finalists," the judge announced. He cleared his throat, then called out the names.

"Good luck, Michelle!" someone called out.

Michelle turned around. Her friend, Lee Wagner, from school waved at her. He was wearing his Boy Scout uniform.

Jeff Farrington was with him. "Save us a slice!" he joked.

Michelle crossed her fingers on both hands. "Please, please, please . . ." she whispered.

Danny slipped his arm around her shoulders. "Don't worry, pumpkin," he whispered. "I have a good feeling about this one."

Good feeling? Michelle thought. Oh, wow. Her dad thought she was crossing her fingers hoping to win. But she wasn't. She was hoping their names *weren't* called!

They announced three names that Michelle didn't know. Then the judges called out Rachel and her father.

Michelle saw Rachel hug her dad.

Michelle felt sick inside. Rachel would never let her forget it if the Tillys beat the Tanners. Everyone at school would hear about it. Fourth grade would be an awful year!

But that's way better than winning by cheating, Michelle reminded herself.

"And last but not least . . ." the judge shouted.

Michelle wished with all her heart: Don't call our names, don't call our names, please, please, don't call our—

"Danny and Michelle Tanner!"

Michelle's heart sank as her dad cheered. As her family crowded around them, clapping and laughing and shouting.

"We're so proud of you!" Aunt Becky cried. She gave Michelle a big hug.

Michelle glanced at her father. He looked so happy.

It was out of her hands now. There was no turning back.

Across the tent she spotted Rachel glaring at her. "You can't win," she mouthed.

You're telling me! Michelle thought sadly. No matter what happened, she was going to be a big loser either way.

Everyone stood quietly as the judges examined the top five pies. They looked closely at each pie. Sniffed each pie. And finally tasted each pie. Then they met in a huddle on one side of the tent.

Danny squeezed Michelle's hand.

Then Michelle saw Rachel push to the front of the crowd. She had a strange look on her face.

What is Rachel doing? Michelle wondered.

"Judges!" Rachel called out. "Look!"

Michelle felt her stomach flip.

Perfect Rachel swept her perfect long brown hair over her shoulder. She pointed at the table. At one of the pies.

At Michelle and Danny's pie.

"That pie is a fake!" she shouted.

The crowd gasped. The judges frowned.

"What do you mean?" the head judge demanded.

"Can't you tell?" Rachel exclaimed. "It's a store-bought pie."

Michelle gulped. Her heart began to pound.

"How do you know it's from a store?" the judge asked.

"Because," Rachel declared. "This pie is from my dad's bakery!"

Chapter 10

♥ "This pie is from my dad's bakery!" Rachel repeated.

Gasps filled the room. The contest ground to a halt.

Michelle felt a hot blush creep up her neck and spread across her cheek. She had no idea the pie was from Mr. Tilly's bakery!

"That's ridiculous!" Danny cried. "I would never enter a store-bought pie. I don't even serve store-bought pies at home! I always bake from scratch."

Michelle was horrified. This was turning into her worst nightmare!

"You're making very serious charge, young lady," the head judge said to Rachel. "Do you have any proof?"

Rachel pointed to the pie. "See the top?" she asked.

Michelle saw a small slit in the crust. She hadn't paid much attention to that when she bought it. She was in a big hurry.

"It's a vent for steam," Rachel explained.

So what does that prove? Michelle thought. She and her dad had put slits on their first pie. It was to allow steam to escape so the crust wouldn't crack. She looked around. Most of the other pies had some kind of cut in the crust, too.

"But see?" Rachel went on. "It's in the shape of a T—for Tilly. My dad puts that on all his pies."

Michelle's heart sank at the news. She

couldn't believe what a stupid mistake she'd made. She couldn't believe that she tried to cheat.

Danny stepped toward the table. Michelle could tell that her father was insulted. He reached for the pie.

Suddenly an old lady shrieked.

Michelle spun around.

A pig bolted into the tent—Curly Sue! Cassie, Mandy, and Karlee followed close behind.

Michelle leaped toward the pig, too.

But Curly Sue was too fast. She ran straight for the judges' table. Straight for Danny!

"Whhhoooa!" Danny cried as Curly Sue knocked into him. The fake pie fell to the floor with a splat.

"Oink-oink!"

Before anyone could stop her, Curly Sue made a pig of herself. She gobbled up the whole pie.

"Oh, no!" someone exclaimed.

"How awful!" another person cried.

"Thank goodness the pig ate the evidence," Michelle muttered under her breath. But not softly enough.

"Evidence?" Michelle's father asked. "What do you mean, *evidence?*"

Chapter
11

♥ Michelle peeked out through her straw-berry-blond bangs at her father. "That's what I tried to tell you, Dad. Right before the judging started."

Michelle slipped her hand around her father's arm and pulled him toward a corner of the tent.

She took a deep breath. Then she blurted out the whole story. How she ruined their wonderful pie trying to make it better. How she tried to make another pie in secret at

Cassie's house. And how she finally stooped to cheating by buying a pie at a bakery.

"B-but, Michelle—" Danny sputtered. "I can't believe . . . Why would you . . . ?"

"Dad, I'm sorry," Michelle cut in. "I know now I was wrong. That's what I was trying to tell you when I ran into the tent a few minutes ago. Remember? That's why I wanted to pull our pie out of the contest."

Danny Tanner sighed and ran a hand through his neatly trimmed dark hair. "Oh, Michelle—"

"I'm so sorry," she said again. "I—I got mixed up. I knew how important it was to you to win the contest. I wanted that blue ribbon so much. I wanted my picture in the photo album with you. Just like D.J. and Stephanie. I didn't want to be the only loser in the family. I . . . I didn't want to let you down."

Michelle stared at the toes of her sneakers, waiting for her father to holler at her. She was ready for it. She knew she deserved it.

But her father didn't say anything.

Michelle glanced up.

What she saw on his face wasn't anger. It looked more like he was . . . sad. He was disappointed in her. That was even worse.

Michelle buried her face in her father's arms. "Oh, Dad, I'm so sorry—"

Danny sighed. "I'm sorry, too."

Michelle looked up, confused. "You are?"

Danny kneeled down so they were eye to eye. "I'm sorry I put so much pressure on you to win that blue ribbon." He shook his head. "This contest is supposed to be fun. A chance for us to spend time together. It shouldn't just be about winning."

Michelle hugged her father. "I wanted to make you happy. I wanted to make you proud of me."

"You do, Michelle," her father said. "Every day. And you don't need a blue ribbon for that. You do it just by being you."

Michelle grabbed her dad's hand. Together they walked back to the judges' stand.

Karlee caught Curly Sue. The pig's little snout was covered with pie crumbs. But that was all that was left of Michelle's phony pie.

"Sorry, Michelle." Karlee quickly led the pig out of the tent. Cassie and Mandy hurried over to stand with Lee and Jeff.

"Now we can't even be in the contest," Michelle said to her dad. "If only I'd told you everything earlier. We could have made another pie ourselves. Now we're going to miss the whole thing."

"Not true," Danny said with a sly smile. "Your old dad still has a few tricks up his sleeve."

"What are you talking about?" Michelle asked.

"You'll see," Danny replied. "Come on!"

Chapter
12

♥ Danny led Michelle over to the side of the tent. He opened the little red cooler that they had used to carry the fake pie.

Then Danny reached inside and pulled out—

Another pie!

A pie that looked just like the one Michelle had smashed.

"Where did that come from?" Michelle gasped.

"Remember how our recipe made enough

dough and filling for two pies?" he reminded her.

"Yes, but I looked for that when I ruined the first one," Michelle told him. "I thought you threw it out."

"No way! After you went to bed that night, I decided to bake it up," Danny explained. "I got nervous about the contest. You never know what might happen. So I made a second pie. Better safe than sorry, you know."

"But where was it?" Michelle asked. "I didn't see another pie on top of the refrigerator."

"That's because Joey and Uncle Jesse came in drooling all over it. I had to hide it so they wouldn't eat it."

"Where did you hide it?" Michelle asked.

"At Miss Teasdale's house, down the street."

Michelle laughed. "Good thinking!"

Danny glanced up at the judges. They had straightened the table and quieted the crowd.

"If we hurry, maybe we can still enter this pie in the contest."

Michelle studied the pie. "But does it still count in the father-daughter contest if you baked it without me?"

"Sure," her father replied. "After all, you helped mix the dough and the filling. And don't forget—you're the one who came up with our secret ingredient." He leaned down to whisper in her ear. "To add apple juice to the crust."

"May I have your attention, please!" the head judge shouted. "We apologize for the interruption. Let's go on with the father-daughter apple-pie-baking competition. Since the Tanner pie has been—er, eaten—we'll proceed with our four finalists."

"Excuse me," Danny called out. He hurried to the judges' table carrying the second pie. "We have a spare. Made from our original recipe. Can we still enter it in the contest?"

The judges whispered together a moment. Then the head judge said, "There is still the matter of this young lady's accusation."

Michelle glanced at Rachel.

Rachel grinned at Michelle.

The judge asked Danny, "Is this pie store-bought, or did you bake it yourself?"

"We definitely baked it ourselves. See?" Danny held the pie up. "This one is in Grandma Tanner's old pie plate."

Michelle looked at the pie plate. It was dented and looked a hundred years old. And to Michelle, it was beautiful.

Danny laid the pie on the judges' table.

Rachel stepped forward to take a closer look. She scowled when she saw the top of the pie. There was no T shape cut into the crust. Just several small holes in a circle shape.

Rachel's father came up behind her and glanced at the pie. He frowned at his daughter. "This pie is not from my bakery," he said to the judges. Then he and Rachel went back to their places in the crowd.

Michelle squeezed her father's hand as the judging continued. Their real pie looked nice. But the pie baked by Rachel and her dad looked so fancy and special. Who would win?

The judges cut a final slice from each pie. They tasted each one. They made notes and whispered among themselves. Michelle thought the judging would take forever! Cassie and Mandy waved at her and crossed their fingers in the air.

At last the judges made their decision. The head judge cleared his throat. "Third place—and a green ribbon—goes to . . . Jonas and Becca Thompson!"

The crowd applauded. Michelle clapped, too. But she was worried. She'd been too upset earlier to look at the other pies. The Thompsons' pie looked really pretty.

"Second place—and a red ribbon—goes to . . ."

Michelle held her breath.

"Jim and Rachel Tilly!"

The crowd clapped as Rachel and her father stepped forward. Mr. Tilly looked pleased. But Rachel's face twisted into a pout.

Michelle glanced quickly at the other pies. The Tanner pie could never win if the fancy Tilly pie took second place. Did one of the remaining pies have something special in it? Chocolate chips? Diamond rings?

The judge smiled and picked up the blue ribbon. "And the blue ribbon for best apple pie in the father-daughter category goes to . . ."

Michelle squeezed her eyes shut.

"Danny and Michelle Tanner!"

Her family exploded into cheers around her. Michelle felt her father take her hand and lead her to the judges' table.

She couldn't believe it! They won!

"Congratulations," the head judge said as he pinned the ribbon onto the pie. Then he

addressed the crowd. "There were many wonderful pies in this contest today. Some
unusual. Some beautiful. But the Tanners' pie
just plain tasted the best. It had a strong old-
fashioned apple flavor—like an apple pie
Grandma might have made."

Michelle giggled. Grandma did! she
thought.

"In our opinion," the judge continued, "it
was absolutely perfect."

The crowd applauded again. Rachel and her
father came by to congratulate them.

"We'll have to get together and talk
recipes," Mr. Tilly said, clapping Danny on
the back.

He seems awful nice, Michelle thought,
considering he's Rachel's dad.

"Congratulations, Michelle," Rachel said
loud enough for everyone can hear. Then she
whispered, "I don't know what you did,
Michelle Tanner. But there was something

fishy about this whole thing. And believe me, I'm not going to forget it!"

Rachel smiled up at her father and said in a perfectly sweet voice, "Let's go, Daddy. I want to get some cotton candy." She dragged her father away.

"Quick!" Aunt Becky cried. She pulled out her camera. "We need to take your picture while the glow of victory still shines on your faces!"

Michelle laughed as she stood up straight and tall with her father. They held the pie between them. Michelle made sure the blue ribbon would show.

Flash! Flash! Flash!

Aunt Becky and D.J. took several more pictures.

Dots swam before Michelle's eyes from all the flashes. But she didn't mind. She was too happy.

"I can't wait to put this in the family

album," Danny told Michelle. "Grandma Tanner would have been proud. And so am I. Michelle, you are the apple of my eye!"

The lunchroom buzzed with excitement the next Monday at school. Cassie had won second prize in the bubble-blowing contest. And Mandy came in first for her pig calling.

"Congratulations, Michelle," Lee Wagner said. He sat down next to her. "Got anything good to trade for lunch?"

"She has her dad's famous chocolate chip cookies," Mandy replied.

"I'd trade my whole lunch for just *one* of those cookies." Lee licked his lips. "They're awesome!"

"*My* chocolate chip cookies are much better than Mi-*chelle's*." Rachel walked over to the table. "They're from my dad's bakery. You should trade with *me* instead."

Cassie rolled her eyes. "Now that she lost

the apple pie contest, Rachel's never going to stop trying to beat you."

"Well, let's look on the bright side," Michelle said with a small grin. "With Rachel around, fourth grade will never be boring."

YOU COULD WIN A COOL SLEEPOVER PARTY!

FULL HOUSE™
Michelle

1 Grand Prize

A sleepover party for the winner and four friends. Each friend gets a sleeping bag, a video, a CD, a backpack and a T-shirt from the Warner Bros. Studio Store and a copy of the newest FULL HOUSE: MICHELLE book from Minstrel® Books—plus loads of party provisions to keep you going all night like pizza, soda, and cupcakes!

Send your entry with your name, age, address, phone number, and parent's (or legal guardian's) signature for permission to enter the FULL HOUSE: MICHELLE/SLEEPOVER PARTY Sweepstakes to:

Pocket Books/FULL HOUSE: MICHELLE/
SLEEPOVER PARTY Sweepstakes,
1230 Avenue of the Americas, 13th Floor, New York, NY 10020

Name _____

Age _____

Address _____

City _____ State _____

Zip Code _____

Phone Number(_____)_____

Parent's (or Legal Guardian's) Signature

_____

(see next page for official rules)

Pocket Books/FULL HOUSE: MICHELLE/SLEEPOVER PARTY Sweepstakes Official Rules:

1. NO PURCHASE NECESSARY. Enter by mailing the completed Official Entry Form (no copies allowed) or by mailing a 3 x 5 card on which you have included your name, age, address, phone number, and your parent's (or legal guardian's) signature for permission to enter the FULL HOUSE: MICHELLE/SLEEPOVER PARTY Sweepstakes to Pocket Books/FULL HOUSE: MICHELLE/SLEEPOVER PARTY Sweepstakes, 1230 Avenue of the Americas, 13th Floor, New York, NY 10020. Sweepstakes begins September 1, 1999. All entries must be postmarked by 2/1/2000 and received by 2/10/2000. Not responsible for lost, late, damaged, stolen, illegible, mutilated, incomplete, postage-due, misdirected or not delivered entries or for typographical errors in the entry form or rules. Entries are void if they are in whole or in part illegible, incomplete or damaged. You may enter as often as you wish, but each entry must be mailed separately. One entry per envelope. No entries will be returned. Winners will be selected at random from all eligible entries received in a drawing to be held on or about February 15, 2000. Winners will be notified by mail.

2. Prizes: 1 Grand Prize: A sleepover party for winner and four friends which will include five sleeping bags from Warner Bros. Studio Store, five videos from Warner Bros. Studio Store, five CDs from Warner Bros. Studio Store, five backpacks from Warner Bros. Studio Store, five T-shirts from Warner Bros. Studio Store, five copies of the latest FULL HOUSE: MICHELLE book from Minstrel Books, and party provisions such as pizza, soda, and cupcakes (approx. retail value: $700.00)

3. The sweepstakes is open to legal residents of the U.S. and Canada (excluding Quebec), ages 14 or younger (as of February 1, 2000). Void in Puerto Rico and wherever prohibited or restricted by law. All federal, state and local laws apply. Family members and those living in the same household employees of Warner Bros. and Parachute Properties and Parachute Press, Inc. (individually and collectively "Parachute") and Simon & Schuster, Inc. and their respective officers, directors, shareholders, suppliers, parents, subsidiaries, affiliates, agencies, sponsors, participating retailers, professional representatives, and persons connected with the use, marketing or conduct of this sweepstakes are not eligible.

4. The odds of winning depend upon the number of eligible entries received.

5. If the winner is a Canadian resident, then he/she must correctly answer a skill-based question administered by mail in order to receive the prize.

6. All expenses on receipt and use of prize including federal, state and local taxes are the sole responsibility of the winner. Winner's parent or (legal guardian) will be required to execute and return an Affidavit of Eligibility and Liability/Publicity release and all other legal documents which the sweepstakes sponsor may require within 15 days of notification attempt or an alternate winner will be selected.

7. Winner's parent (or legal guardian) on behalf of winner grants to Simon & Schuster and Parachute the right to use the winner's name, photograph and likeness for any advertising, promotion, publicity, or any other purpose without further compensation or permission except where prohibited by law. No cash substitution, transfer, or assignment of prize allowed, except by sponsor for reason of unavailability in which case a prize of equal or greater value will be awarded.

8. By participating in this sweepstakes, entrants agree to be bound by these rules and the decisions of the judges and sweepstakes sponsors, which are final in all matters relating to the sweepstakes. Failure to comply with the official rules may result in a disqualification of your entry and prohibition of any further participation in this sweepstakes.

9. Winner's parent (or legal guardian) on winner's behalf agree that the sweepstakes sponsors and their respective officers, directors, shareholders, employees, suppliers, parent companies, subsidiaries, affiliates agencies, sponsors, participating retailers, professional representatives, and persons connected with the use, marketing, or conduct of this sweepstakes shall have no responsibility or liability for any injury, loss or damage of any kind arising out of participation in this sweepstakes or the acceptance or use of the prize.

10. For the name of the prize winners (available after 3/1/00), send a stamped, self-addressed envelope to Prize Winner, Pocket Books/FULL HOUSE: MICHELLE/ SLEEPOVER PARTY Sweepstakes, 1230 Avenue of the Americas, 13th Floor New York, NY 10020.   2303 (2 of 2)

FULL HOUSE™

SISTERS

A brand-new series starring Stephanie AND Michelle!

#1 Two On The Town

Stephanie and Michelle find themselves
in the big city—and in big trouble!

#2 One Boss Too Many

Stephanie and Michelle think camp will be major fun.
If only these two sisters were getting along!

When sisters get together...expect the unexpected!

A MINSTREL® BOOK
Published by Pocket Books

2012-01